Disney PRINCESS

palace pets

Pet Friends Forever!

By Andrea Posner-Sanchez
Illustrated by the Disney Storybook Art Team

A Random House PICTUREBACK® Book

Random House 🏠 New York

randomhouse.com/kids
ISBN 978-0-385-38786-6
MANUFACTURED IN CHINA
10 9 8 7 6

PFF = Pet Friends Forever!

The Palace Pets are all so sweet and adorable. That's why the princesses love them—and that's why they make terrific friends. With a Palace Pet, you're getting a BFF who's also a PFF!

Each pet has different likes and talents, but they all love spending time with their royal friends.

Meet Treasure!

Unlike most cats, Treasure loves water! When she's not splashing in the waves or riding in a sailboat, you can find Treasure relaxing in a bubble bath!

Fun Fact:
Treasure's fur always smells like a fresh sea breeze.

Favorite Thing:
Her collection of seashells and trinkets.

Meet Teacup!

Teacup is one talented pup!
She's a born performer who loves
putting on a show—and hearing
applause from her audience.

Fun Fact:

Teacup can balance a teacup on her head while standing on her hind legs!

Favorite Thing:

The sunglasses Belle gave her.

Meet Blondie!

This little pony has big dreams to be part of the kingdom's royal guard. Blondie has already perfected saluting and looking regal!

Fun Fact:
Blondie marched in a parade by sneaking in next to the royal horses.

Favorite Thing:
The ribbon Rapunzel tied around the braid in her mane.

Meet Pumpkin!

Whenever Pumpkin hears music, she just
has to dance! This glamorous puppy loves
to twirl and hop and prance about.

Favorite Thing:
Her royal bed.

Meet Berry!

Sweet Berry is a shy bunny with a sweet tooth! Her little nose twitches with excitement when she smells fruit and treats of all kinds.

Ballroom Beauty

Purrlicious

Royal Pony

Pretty Kitty

© Disney

Fun Fact:
Berry hid inside a pail of blueberries at Snow White's castle.

Favorite Thing:
Blueberries!

Meet Beauty!

The prettiest kitten in all the land is also the sleepiest! Beauty loves to curl up and take a nap just about anywhere.

Fun Fact:
Princess Aurora's singing always helps Beauty fall asleep.

Favorite Thing:
The treats Prince Phillip brings her when she wakes from her naps.

Perfect Pairs!

Each lovely pet found her way
into the heart—and home—
of a princess. Here's how:

ARIEL & TREASURE

Hoping for some adventure on the high seas, Treasure stowed away on Prince Eric's ship. One day, Ariel came aboard and discovered the red-haired kitten. Before long, they became the best of friends. Ariel and Treasure love swimming together and collecting shells and other trinkets on the beach.

BELLE & TEACUP

Teacup was performing her amazing balancing act when a beam of sunlight reflected off one of Belle's earrings and shone in the puppy's eyes. The teacup fell off the pup's head and broke. Belle kindly picked up the broken pieces and carried them—and Teacup—home with her. Now Teacup loves performing in the palace for her royal best friend!

RAPUNZEL & BLONDIE

A parade was being held to celebrate Rapunzel's return to the kingdom. Blondie sneaked in and began proudly marching along with the royal horses—until she tripped on her long mane! Rapunzel rushed to comfort the pony and couldn't resist braiding her beautiful mane. Blondie saluted to thank the princess. Now Blondie is proud to be Rapunzel's personal royal pony!

CINDERELLA & PUMPKIN

The Prince wanted to surprise Cinderella with a special gift for their first anniversary—and that gift was Pumpkin! As soon as the princess spotted the dancing, prancing puppy on her balcony, they became the best of friends. Pumpkin and Cinderella love attending royal balls, where they dance together all night long!

AURORA & BEAUTY

While strolling through the castle gardens, Aurora and the good fairies noticed a pink kitten sleeping in the grass. When Beauty awoke, she didn't hiss or run away. She simply leaped into Aurora's arms—and soon fell back to sleep. Beauty and Aurora love snuggling up together and napping, no matter what time of day it is!

SNOW WHITE & BERRY

Snow White discovered Berry while she was out picking blueberries for a pie. The princess shared some of her berries with the shy bunny and then headed home. But the hungry bunny followed Snow White—and the big bucket of berries!— to her castle. Now Berry and the princess enjoy many sweet treats together every day!

PFF Quiz

Take this fun quiz and then turn
the page to see which Palace Pet
is your perfect PFF.

1. **What do you most like to do on the weekend?**
   A. Sleep late—then have a yummy breakfast.
   B. Eat a ton of fruits and veggies.
   C. Go to the salon to get your hair braided.
   D. Perform in a talent show.
   E. Take a dance class.
   F. Go swimming.

2. Where would you go on your dream vacation?
   A. Any hotel with a comfortable bed.
   B. Paris, so you can taste how French chefs cook carrots.
   C. Buckingham Palace, so you can salute the guards.
   D. Circus camp, to learn new skills.
   E. On a cruise ship with a huge dance floor.
   F. A seaside resort, so you can swim in the ocean.

3. When you go to a friend's house, what is the first thing you do?
   A. Lounge on the couch.
   B. Peek in the fridge and ask for a snack.
   C. Greet her parents with a salute.
   D. Put on a show, complete with costumes and props.
   E. Turn on some music and dance.
   F. Ask if she has a pool.

Quiz Results

If you picked mainly As—
Beauty is your perfect Palace Pet!
You can cuddle up together for catnaps.

If you picked mainly Bs—
Berry is your perfect Palace Pet!
You can eat sweet pies and crunchy
salads together.

If you picked mainly Cs—
Blondie is your perfect Palace Pet!
You can braid her mane while you
watch parades.

If you picked mainly Ds—
Teacup is your perfect Palace Pet!
The two of you can put on performances
for your family and friends.

If you picked mainly Es—
Pumpkin is your perfect Palace Pet!
You can hold dance parties every day.

If you picked mainly Fs—
Treasure is your perfect Palace Pet!
You can hit the beach or the pool and
splash around together.

If you picked all different letters—
Any Palace Pet would love to hang out
and have fun with you!